First published in Great Britain
in 2019 by Andersen Press Ltd.,
20 Vauxhall Bridge Road,
London SW1V 2SA.
Copyright © Tony Ross, 2019
The right of Tony Ross to be identified
as the author and illustrator of this work
has been asserted by him in accordance with
the Copyright, Designs and Patents Act, 1988.
Printed and bound in Malaysia.
First edition.
British Library Cataloguing in Publication Data available.
ISBN 978 1 78344 7817

Silly
Mr Wolf

Tony Ross

ANDERSEN PRESS

Mr Wolf did not always tell the truth.
He was tricky.

Years ago, he would dress up as a sheep, and try to be their worst friend.

But when he grew up, the sheep's clothing was far too small for him.

So nowadays, if he wanted a nice, plump sheep for his dinner, he put a bag over his head so no one would know that he was a wolf, then he lied about his name.

"My name is Mr Jones," he said to a
sheep with dinner written all over him.
"Will you walk with me?"

Of course, that sheep was never seen again.
Very soon, the sheep began to understand,
and they feared Mr Jones as well as Mr Wolf.

Mother sheep used to tell their lambs, "Don't go near Mr Wolf, he is a bad'un. That goes for Mr Jones, too. Go near them, and you will never be seen again."

Of course, the lambs knew that mother sheep are very wise, so they kept well away from Mr Wolf and Mr Jones.

That being the case, the sheep, with their lambs,
lived happily and Mr Wolf lived HUNGRILY!

He tried to catch a sheep for dinner,
but as soon as they saw the paper
bag and the long grey tail, they
knew exactly who it was.

"Run for your lives!" they bleated, "It's Mr Wolf!"
"Or Mr Jones!" cried others.

The sheep did run for their lives,
and Mr Wolf went hungry.

"This is no good!" snarled Mr Wolf to himself.
"I must become someone else,
someone they don't know."
Mr Wolf put on a new suit and
a bigger paper bag on his head.

"Hello, sheep," he smiled. "I am not a wolf, I am Mr Smith." The sheep smiled back. "It's good that you are not a wolf, Mr Smith," they said. "Welcome."

Mr Wolf pounced and stuffed a sheep into his dinner bag. He went hungry no more.

When the wisest sheep noticed that they were getting fewer and fewer, he understood what was going on, and explained it all to the others. So now, the sheep kept well away from Mr Wolf AND Mr Jones, AND Mr Smith.

When Mr Wolf was ready for another
sheepy supper, he put on different
clothes and a bigger paper bag.

"Hello," he purred.
"I'm Mr Thomson,
I'm not a wolf."

"That's OK then," smiled the
sheep, until Mr Wolf pounced.

The sheep agreed, it was
time for a very serious talk.

"We must get sticks to drive away
Mr Wolf," said the wisest sheep.
"That's the idea!" agreed the others, and
they picked up large and dangerous sticks.

There was, though, one old sheep who disagreed.
"Yes, we can whack Mr Wolf, but what
about all the others?" he asked.
"What others?" cried the rest of the sheep.

"Well, his friends, Mr Jones, and Mr Smith, and Mr Thomson. There are four of them! We cannot drive away FOUR wolves."

So the sheep dropped their sticks and ran away. Mr Wolf could not follow them, because of the paper bag on his head. He didn't think of taking it off.

Silly. Silly. Silly. Silly. Silly Mr Wolf.

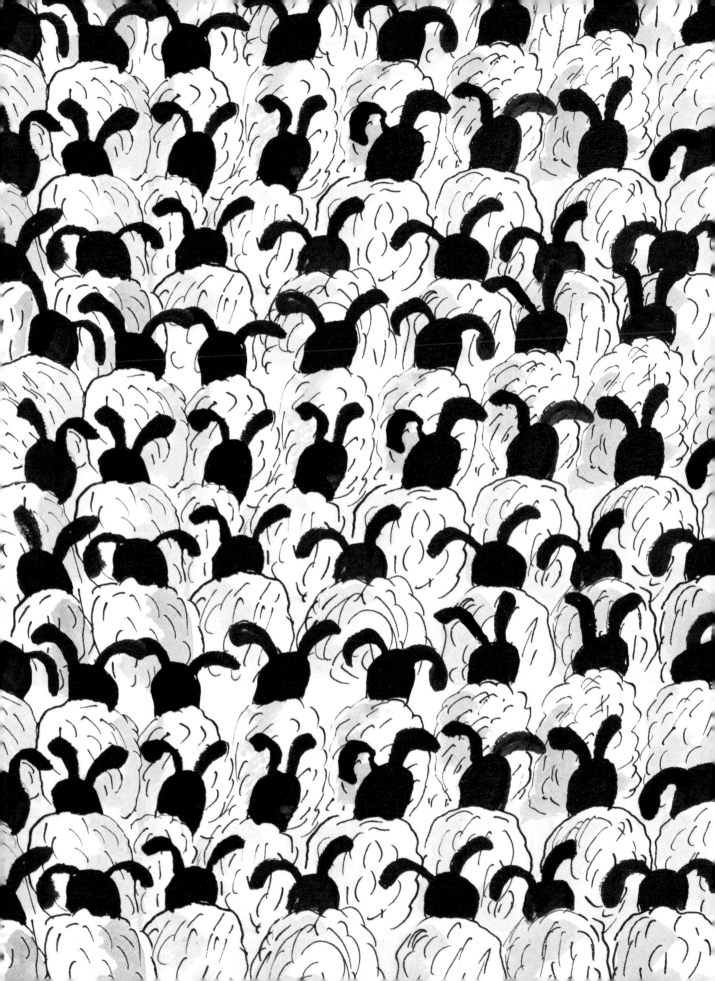